A Hesitant Bri
Older Hor

By
Faith Johnson

Seasons of Love - The Winter Mail
Order Bride Series

Table of Contents

Few Unsolicited Testimonials for my books 4

FREE GIFT 5

Story Begins 6

FREE GIFT 91

Please Check out My Other Works 92

Thank You 93

Few Unsolicited Testimonials for my books

By

Format: Kindle Edition

Five DETERMINED Stars! This short story "Mail Order Bride-The Rancher's Runaway Bride" by Faith Johnson in the "Brave Frontier Bride" series tells the tale of Dora who has a problem. Back east, her dad wants to marry her off to clear a business debt, and she wants to escape to wed a Wyoming rancher. But after her decision and relocation, she has only made matters much worst in this story with an unusual twist and ending. Highly Recommended. **Five DECISIVE Stars**

By
Glaidene's reads, Format: Kindle Edition
Another good mail order bride story. I enjoyed this story , it helps people to improve their lives and the lives of others by being impartial . Enough for now I hope you will read and enjoy this story!!!!!

By
Laura Lee ,   Format: Kindle Edition
In the Mail order bride series, the story of a lost baby for the Widowed Bride, part of frontier Babies, which is well-written by author Faith Johnson and is an exciting must-read story

FREE GIFT

Just to say thanks for purchasing my book, I'd like to gift you a Best Selling FREE Mail Order Bride Audiobook
<u>100% FREE!</u>

Please GO TO

<u>http://cleanromancepublishing.com/mobgift</u>

And get your FREE gift

Thanks for being such a wonderful client.

Story Begins

Chapter One-The Journey Begins

Fiona shifted uneasily as she settled inside the coach alongside several other passengers. She was leaving for Hill County, Montana at last. Pulling the thin shawl tightly around herself, she tried to keep a cool composure despite her tumultuous feelings.

It had been quite a task for her to make getaway plans without her father's knowledge. Having lost her mother to disease several years ago, most of her life had been spent helping him around their small farm. Father spent most of his time tending to his crops, even though there was not much yield. Her chores were mainly to ensure the smooth running of the place and to offer him company. He was a good man who had done a good job bringing her up singlehandedly, and a wave of guilt crossed her mind at the thought of what his reaction would be when he found out she was gone.

The coach driver announced their departure. Looking around one last time, she pushed back the tears threatening to spill from her eyes. She had no idea when she would be back home to visit, and the thought of leaving familiar surroundings made her nervous. Nevertheless, she put on a brave face, silently hoping for better things ahead.

Soon, they were well on their way, and for some time she stared at the passing landscape. Eventually, though, her mind wandered back to her father, who might now be noticing her quick departure.

She whispered a silent prayer for father's safety. He was a strong man, and would learn to carry on without her. It was time for her to leave home to get started on her own life, and her choice was to join her friends who had headed out to Hill

County, Montana to be mail order brides to men out there. She thought of the man who awaited her on the end of the journey—a complete stranger to her.

From the few letters the two had, exchanged James seemed like the ideal husband for her. He had managed to woo her with stories about how the two of them would live happily together once she made it over. In her mind's eye, she pictured a tall man full of virility and strength, with handsome looks, too. Letting out a sigh, Fiona kept picturing him in her mind's eye.

As the days went by, the scenery began to change. The rolling hills were replaced with long stretches of prairie grass. The coach was going faster now despite the bumpy mud road stretching erratically ahead of them. The cool wind blowing made her hunch into her seat in a bid to keep off the cold. Fiona had her head covered with a hat, her long hair held in one long braid. Her flawless skin flushed rose with the cold, and her eyes peeked from under her hat with a calm cool. She had inherited both her mother's good looks and father's stately demeanor, though now she was a bit nervous about what her new life would bring.

The coach slowed to a stop at her destination as darkness settled over the plains. It was the start of winter in Montana, and she felt the biting cold hit her face. It had been a long journey due to the snow that made progress slow, and she was looking forward to the end of it. Since it had been warmer back home, she had not worn anything to keep off the winter cold.

Stepping out of the coach, she looked around in an attempt to find James in the dusk. The entire place was white with snow, and she pulled her shawl closer. He had promised to be waiting for her when she arrived. Bag in hand; Fiona stood waiting, heart thumping loudly in her chest. What if her handsome prince had changed his mind, and did not turn out to pick her up? Pushing the thought to the back of her mind, she calmly waited, hoping he would find her soon enough.

Finally, she heard her name called. She turned to look into the handsome eyes of a stranger, tall and with strands of white hair at his temples. He stood smiling down at her, gloved hand held out in greeting.

"You must be Fiona. My name is James Roberts," he said. Despite the cold wind blowing, she felt a spark of warmth go through her when their hands met. Nodding, she let him know he had found her.

"Yes, I am," she barely managed, shivering from the cold. He noticed, and immediately took hold of her bag to head to the buggy.

"Best get you out of here. You seem cold." With that they were on their way to the buggy he had packed close by to begin a new chapter in life.

Chapter Two- Settling In

After the initial surprise upon meeting James, Fiona followed him to the buggy for the ride from the station. At first she was unable to reconcile herself to the fact that this was the man she had been communicating with via mail. She'd expected to meet a young man, but James was certainly nothing close. He had a warmth around him though, and she allowed herself to go along with him. She had little choice, after all, alone and in a strange land.

It was difficult to maneuver through the road covered with snow, and several times the buggy almost came to a skid. James seemed to know his way around well, and pointed out interesting landmarks along the road to their destination.

"You must be worn out after travelling. I will take you to my sister's house, where you will stay until we get married in a few days."

Thankful she would have time to think things over before committing herself, she nodded courteously, watching him under the brim of her hat. James appeared keen to learn a lot about her quickly, and soon they were chatting away. When he pulled up in front of an old farmhouse, she peered into the dark for a sight of her destination.

The entire place was covered with snow, making it seem magical in the light from the front porch. "Here we are at last. I am sure Charlotte has a hot meal awaiting you in there," he said out, helping her with the bag. Watching him walk ahead of her, Fiona realized that he seemed fit despite his age. Broad shoulders highlighted in the dim light, he turned around to usher her in to the house. They were met by a matronly looking middle-aged woman who came out, arms outstretched to greet her.

"Finally I get to meet the beauty my brother picked for a wife! Welcome home dear, make yourself comfortable," the woman said, looking her over. James stepped in to make introductions, his arms draped fondly around each of the women. "This is girl I told you about, Charlotte. She has come over to be my wife and will stay here until we are married. Fiona, meet my sister, Charlotte. The two of us only have each other, having lost both our parents a while ago."

"You must be cold, you poor dear. Come on in, I have a warm bath waiting for you. You should feel better after you take it," Charlotte told her enthusiastically.

The warmth of the house made her feel welcome, and she headed for a bath before going to dinner. Soft laughter filtered through the house as she cleaned up for dinner. Feeling relaxed after her bath, but still trying hard to reconcile her thoughts to getting married to a much older man, she sighed as she headed to the living room.

"There is my beautiful bride. I am sure you feel much better now," James called out when he saw her. Hair brushed and held in a chignon, she had a fresh look about her.

"Yes, I do," she told him, a smile playing on her lips. He held her gaze for a while, and she lowered her eyes as she blushed. For a moment there was tension between the two, which was thankfully broken by Charlotte's call for grace before the meal. They bowed their heads in prayer, then Charlotte proceeded to dish out generous portions of food onto their plates.

"Oh no, you will kill me with all this food someday," James joked to his sister. Watching the two of them, Fiona thought how much they enjoyed each other's company.

"Quite a welcome thought, that one. I might try to do just that, you know," Charlotte said with a smile.

They ate, digging into the roast potatoes and large helpings of veal. Charlotte had made the special meal for her, something Fiona appreciated very much. When they were done, James stood to go, thanking his hostess just as Charlotte's husband, Bobby, walked in to the house. The plump farmer affectionately called out greetings before going to freshen up for dinner.

"And who is the beautiful lady with us tonight?" Bobby inquired upon seeing Fiona.
"Have you forgotten already? This is Fiona, James's bride from the East," Charlotte responded.
 His face lit up and he extended a hand in greeting.
"I am so pleased to meet you. You will soon be

family, and are welcome here for as long as it takes."

It was so easy for her to fit in with these people, as they all went out of their way to ensure she felt welcome. However, she was worn out from the long hours on the road, and Fiona thanked her hosts before asking to retire to bed early.

"You go right ahead, dear. You must be tired after the trip," Charlotte told her.

The older woman walked Fiona to her room to ensure she was comfortable before leaving her to sleep. Her room was fashioned with warm, inviting colors, making it the kind of place she would enjoy being alone with her thoughts. After Charlotte left, she stood looking out of the window at the land that stretched to the horizon, all covered with snow.

Images of James stayed in her mind as she lay down in bed. He might not be what she'd expected, yet there was definitely something very attractive about the man she was promised to. Thinking back to the moment their eyes met across the room, she felt a strange thrill, and shivered.

Perhaps it is the cold, she reckoned. Only she knew that was far from the reason. Stranger to these kinds of emotions, she would have to wait to find out why he made her feel that way.
Finally after struggling to keep awake, she yielded to sleep.

Chapter Three- Revelation Time

Life settled into a routine after the first few days. With plenty to do around the farm, Fiona hardly had time to get bored. She enjoyed helping out in the kitchen as the two women made different dishes together. Occasionally, when it did not snow too much, they went out to the fields.

"You know, you are just like the sister I always wished for," Charlotte told her while they did the dishes together. Fiona liked the older woman, too, even though it was only a few days after the two met. She wanted to ask about James but held back, not wanting to sound too forthright. It was

Charlotte however, who volunteered information about her brother to her.
"You know, I thought James would never marry again after he lost his wife at childbirth," she said, watching Fiona's face for a reaction to the news.

Fiona felt her heart lurch at the thought of how that must have felt to him.

So that was why he was alone at an advanced age, she thought.

"That must have been hard for him. Was it a long time ago?"

"Oh, yes, it was. It is over ten years ago since it happened. James had delayed in getting married, and finally settled for a childhood friend of his. A rather sweet girl, the poor thing lost both her life and that of the baby she was delivering. James was inconsolable after that, vowing never to marry again. We were quite happy therefore, when he told us about you."

The information certainly helped clear up some of Fiona's questions. She had wondered about his single state, thinking he should have been married by now. It made sense for him to want to wait, after losing his wife and child. The information certainly made it easier for her to relate with the man who would soon be her husband.

That is, if she could still bring herself to go along with the plan.

James came over to visit every day, each time inquiring if she was ready for the wedding. She wanted more time to get used to the idea, but knew she would have to make up her mind soon enough. But she still had not gotten used to the idea of him being so much older than her.

"You seem to be having second thoughts about getting married to me," he told her one day as they sat on the front yard, late in the afternoon.

Charlotte was out in the back garden gathering vegetables for dinner. Fiona liked living with her, but knew she could not push it too long. She would have to make up her mind about marrying James, so that they could live together as man and wife. She had committed the issue to God in prayer, and was awaiting confirmation it was the right move for her to make.

"A little bit more time and all should be well," she assured him, despite being unsure herself. The thought that she would be marrying a man almost her father's age did not sit very well with her. James was caring, and he would make a good husband and father to her children, but she found herself unable to overcome her doubts about their age difference.

Charlotte came around to find them sitting together, and calling out in a cheery voice, invited them in.

"Oh, you two lovebirds! I am sure you can't wait to get married, can you? Come on in for coffee. You can talk some more over it." Fiona recognized it as a bid to keep them apart for now. They were not supposed to be in any compromising situation before getting married and Charlotte was ensuring they remained chaste. James jumped to his feet, and then reached a hand to help her up. They chatted a bit more over coffee before he took his leave.

Alone in her room later that night, Fiona pondered life being married to James. What she had seen of him so far proved he was ready to settle down with her, but picturing herself as his life partner still proved a challenge to her. Praying for God to reveal his plan, she took out her Bible. A verse jumped out at her.

1 Thessalonians 3:12 May the Lord make your love increase and overflow for each other and for everyone else, just as ours does for you.

Chapter Four-Discovery

Early morning birdsong followed her as she made her way to the local market. Progress was difficult, as she had to skirt around the thick snow all along the way. Charlotte had been wary of letting her go by herself, but she had stubbornly insisted she would make it on her own. Now struggling through the snow, she wished she had waited a little longer for the snow to melt.

Town was already teeming with early morning shoppers, and she made her way to begin her purchases. Suddenly, she heard her name called out, and she wheeled around to come face to face with one of the girls from back East who had travelled to be a mail order bride.

"Imagine meeting you here, what a pleasant surprise!" Lucy shouted at the top of her voice.

Happy to see familiar faces, the two girls hugged warmly, then stepped aside to catch up for a while. "I am so glad to see you too, Lucy. How are you getting on?"

At the question, Lucy's face became serious. "I am not doing too well. The man I left home to come and get married to turned out not so good after all, and I am considering going back home to my parents." Through her tears, Lucy explained to her about the man she married not being faithful, and still chasing after other women.

"I wish I had found a more mature man to marry me. I am done trying to keep track of the man I got married to," she ended her story. There was not much Fiona could do but console her in her situation. It was a chance they took, coming over to get married to strangers in the West. Sad that Lucy's life had turned out that way, she hoped it might be different for her should she marry James.

The two hugged again, and promised to try to meet in town for another visit together.

After the two parted ways, Fiona hurriedly made her purchases before heading back home. On her way, she thought about her friend's predicament. Perhaps it was time she rethought the idea of getting married to an older man. She got back in time to start lunch together with Charlotte. James would be dropping in later, and it was a good time for the two of them to talk.

"You will make a good bride for my brother. You learn fast, look at you going to the market all by yourself already!" Charlotte said in her usual excited manner.
"It was nothing, really. I enjoyed the experience," Fiona smiled.

"I didn't think you would make two steps with all this snow. Looks like I underestimated you."

Fiona laughed at the way the older woman made it sound like she had completed such a feat. She would miss their times together, when it came to time for them to part.

As soon as they were done cooking, she left to go get changed into a flowered dress with a flaring bodice that emphasized her waistline. With her hair held in a bun, she stepped into the living room just as James walked in. For a while the two stared at each other, tension evident between them. It was as if she was seeing him for the first time, and he seemed different in her eyes.

Chapter Five-The Encounter

It was exactly three weeks since her arrival. All that remained was for her to give a nod so the wedding could take place. After seeking God and praying about it, she was sure it was the right thing for her to do. Now all she had to do was to make her intentions known to James so plans could commence.

The biting winter made her long for the sunny days. It would have been better for her wedding to take place at a time when the flowers were out. Growing up back home, she had always envisioned herself having a summer wedding. She would make the best of the situation, though, seeing as she could no longer postpone.

Already she had written to her father back home, informing him of her intentions. She was happy when he wrote back, wishing her all the best in finding happiness in life. Perhaps she would be able to find time to go visit him after she was settled in.

The little white church they attended stood out in the large expanse of land, and Fiona would visit when she could to have some private time with God. The church looked magical in the snow, and when she entered Fiona saw several people already seated. Taking a bench by herself, she started to read her Bible, but was cut short by the entrance of the man she was promised to marry. Distracted from what she was doing, she calmly sat watching him take a seat by himself.

James went to sit at a far corner, and she was so riveted by the sight of him bowed earnestly in prayer that she almost forgot the reason she was there. Something appeared to be on his mind, and his expression was intense. Wishing she could read his moving lips, she continued watching him for some time.

She waited for him to finish before walking up to him. She put a hand on his shoulder, and saw the surprise on his face when he looked up to find her staring down at him. Patting the seat next to her, he invited her to take a seat.

"I had no idea you were here, too. How nice to see you," he said with a smile

"This is where I come to spend some time with God, as well," she said, sitting next to him.
An uncomfortable silence ensued, neither of them knowing what to say next. Their attraction to each other was strong, threatening to derail them both from the thing that had brought them to church. She cleared her throat then, mostly to take attention off the emotions between them.

"I have been meaning to give you my answer to your question about us," she said.

His eyes widened, and he sat upright to give her undivided attention. Stuttering at the start, she found the courage to break the news to him at last.

"I have decided to get married to you. I hope you are still interested," she added hesitantly. Overwhelmed with joy, he checked himself to keep from throwing his arms around her. Instead, he held out his hands to take hers with his own. "That has to be the best news I have heard in a long time. I have been praying you would make that choice."

He led her outside, and together walked into the pastor's office. The chubby man sitting in the office beamed when he saw them, and holding out his hand, gave each a warm handshake.

"Hello, James. Good seeing you here," the pastor said. Taking seats across from each other, the two sat before the man who would join them in marriage.

James spoke up, joy evident in his voice. "Thank you, pastor. This is Fiona, the girl I am getting married to soon. We came over to fix a wedding date with you."

"Is that so? What great news! I am happy you have settled that at last. Tell me, when would you like to have us do the wedding?"

There would be no use waiting any longer, and the wedding was fixed in a week's time, leaving them only few days to prepare. Once settled, they stepped out of the pastor's office, both of them beaming with joy.

Chapter Six-In the Wrong Hands

They had not realized how much time had passed, and dark shadows had started to fall as the happy couple walked back home from the church. As they hurried back to Charlotte's house, James did not notice the people lurking in the shadows along the way. Only when the order for them to stop rang out did he realize they had encountered a gang of outlaws. Fiona let out a scream when one of them pulled at her and yanked her to the side of the road.

"Leave her alone!" he shouted, but the men just laughed roughly.

"Oh, I see you do not want me to lay hands on the little missy. How would you like me to take her with me, instead?" the man holding her shouted at him.

"What do you want from us? We have no money," James said, buying time while looking for a way out.

The man laughed, tugging Fiona closer to him. Fear in her eyes, she looked at James in desperation. Calculating his move, he launched at the two men standing on either side of him. He was a strong man and temporarily destabilized them, but soon they were on their feet, and knocked James to the ground with vicious blows. Suddenly, one of them drew out a gun, prompting Fiona to call out in protest. "Please don't shoot! I will go with you if that's what you want."

That seemed to calm the men, and they started to lead her off with them while the other held the gun on James, preventing him from moving. They had barely taken a few steps, though, when several shots rang out, sending the outlaws scampering in different directions. James leapt to his feet and rushed to Fiona, hugging her tightly.

"Quickly, run to the house while I cover you both."

James recognized Bobby's voice. Easily carrying her off, the two ran as an exchange of shots went on for a while, followed by silence. Back in the house, a frantic Charlotte attended to his wounds while worried about the safety of her husband. "He will be home soon enough. I just know my Bobby will fight his way out of there," she kept saying, as if to convince herself.

Bobby did come home not so long after that, with only a limp from a twisted ankle. Charlotte rushed to his side, feeling him all over for injuries and thankful he was safe. In the stunned silence that followed, they all bowed their heads in a prayer of thanksgiving. Despite having run into outlaws, no one had been hurt, and that was reason enough for them to give thanks.

After the shock had worn off, they fell into animated talk about the incident. Bobby had been out surveying the surroundings when he heard the ensuing scuffle not far off. Gun cocked, he had crept up close to find out what was going on, only to hear James's voice above the din. Quickly making out images of the people involved, he watched Fiona being led off by the outlaws before aiming for the leader of the gang.

"I got him in the leg, causing the others to run for safety," he said.

"Good thing you showed up Bob, as I don't know what might have happened to Fiona here," James said with a shaken voice.

Fiona sat shivering in a corner, trying to come to terms with what had just happened. She might have been captured, had James not put up a fight for her as he did. He had risked his life in the hands of those men, and nothing could assure her more of his love for her.

Charlotte walked to her and put her arms around her to comfort her. It was then that James remembered the good news concerning their upcoming wedding and thought it fit to share.

"Despite all that happened this evening, Fiona and I have some good news to share with you. We are getting married in a week's time."
Charlotte and Bobby offered them both hugs and well wishes.

"God must be on your side as he did not allow those evil men to succeed in their mission on such a joyous day," Bobby said.
Everyone went to bed happy about the good news, despite the day's events. Kneeling on her bedside that evening, Fiona gave thanks to God for his protection over them both. Now all that remained

was to get married to the man who had succeeded in capturing her heart these past few days.

Chapter Seven-The Wedding

With wedding plans in full gear, there was barely time to think of anything else. The entire household was involved in planning for the small ceremony scheduled to take place at the end of the week. Already James had sent out invites to his friends and family, but on such short notice

Fiona's father would not be able to make it, so she would have to make do without any of her relatives at the wedding. Still, she thought Charlotte would fill the gap very well.
It would be a small wedding, only attended by few of their friends. The venue was the little white church they attended every Sunday. Fiona had already fitted the gown passed down generations of the family, and she looked stunning in it.

"That dress looks as if it was made for you! Not much will go into adjusting it to fit you well. I can't wait for James to see you in it on the wedding day," Charlotte said on seeing her try it out.

There were villagers coming over to help with the cooking that Friday evening, and the entire ceremony promised to be exciting for all, despite the cold weather. The house was warm from the fire that burned most of that evening, and Charlotte ran around making certain everything went as it should.

James was also kept busy with preparations, leaving little time to be with Fiona. Yet, each time the two caught sight of each other it was a task to tear away, as there seemed to be a magnet pulling them together.

Not too long now, and soon there will be no holds barred, thought James after one such intense moment.

Fiona kept sending prayers up about the forthcoming marriage to James. Mind set up on making it work out well with the help of God, she had consulted him for wisdom frequently through prayer.

Charlotte had already taken her for a visit to her brother's home not so far away. She was surprised to see the large expanse of land the farmhouse sat on, and noted how well it was kept. Soon it would be her home, the place she shared with her husband once the marriage was solemnized. The thought often filled her with apprehension, since she was green in intimacy matters.

The night before the wedding, James stayed over much later than usual. She caught him throwing curious glances her way, and when it was time for him to leave Bobby called out to her to see him off.

"You better celebrate your last night by yourselves, as by this time tomorrow you two will belong to each another," he teased them.
On the walk to the gate the two were without words, each buried in thoughts of their future together. Clutching his jacket firmly around him to keep out the cold, James seemed reluctant to leave her behind. Only when they were about to part did James speak his mind.

"I can't believe that tomorrow this time you will be my wife," he observed, voice full of emotion. She heard the catch in his voice, and was afraid her own emotions would show if she spoke. They stood regarding each other for a while, afraid of getting carried away by their feelings for one another. Finally, James tore away and, bidding her goodbye, was soon on his way. It was a night filled with anxiety for them both as they looked forward to starting life together the following day.

That Saturday, she got up bright and happy and could hear voices in the living room. Having spent much of the night in thought, she noticed time was well gone and got out of bed. But not before whispering a prayer to God before she left. "Dear God, Please bless my marriage to James," she asked, before a knock on the door cut her short.

"Come in," she called to an excited Charlotte, too anxious to stay away. In high spirits, Charlotte walked in to find out how far along she was in preparing.

"You almost overslept on your wedding! Come on, everyone is here already, waiting to see the bride," Charlotte beamed at her.

"I slept late this morning. I don't know why, but sleep kept evading me for a long time."

"Wedding jitters, that's what it is. Don't worry, it happens to most people," Charlotte offered. "Hurry up now, go take your bath. We don't want to keep the bridegroom waiting too long in church, do we now?" she added with a wink.

On her feet fast, Fiona was done bathing in no time at all. Dressed in her wedding gown with hair held back in a long braid, she caused a stir when she walked into the sitting room. The women stared at her eyes full of admiration and several of them went up to congratulate her on the wedding day.

"You look stunning, my dear sister-in-law. Sure to knock my brother for a loop when he sees you looking like that!" Charlotte said, attracting nods of agreement among the rest of the women. Bobby was waiting outside in the buggy to take her to church where James was waiting for her.

The little white church held more meaning for her that day than it had before. Surrounded with snow, it stood firm against the harsh weather. She had been there frequently, but never had the place held so much meaning as it did then. This was where she would make a life commitment to the man she loved, something she would never forget.

The walk down the aisle where James stood waiting was, to her, the most memorable part of the wedding. Seeing him looking stately in an overcoat as he nervously watched her approach made her heart fill up with love. Finally she stood by his side, as James kept a steady gaze on her, eyes unfaltering even for a moment.

She choked back tears as they exchanged their vows, overcome with happiness. Finally man and wife, the two walked out to wild cheering from those in attendance. The reception was at Bobby and Charlotte's home, where the feasting took place most of the afternoon.

"Finally you are my wife. I can't wait to lose the crowd so I can be alone with you," James whispered as they sat at the table to enjoy their meal. She blushed at the meaning of his words, hoping no one noticed, but couldn't hold back a smile.

Chapter Eight-That Warm Feeling

A week had gone by since the wedding, and already Fiona was settling into married life. Thankful to God for a good man, she was ready to help him achieve success in farming. Already the two had their chores spelled out as she concentrated more around the house and the farm while he took care of the animals. James loved to look after the horses, which he bred for sale. Well known in the area for his horseman skills, he looked forward to expanding his business by adding onto the eight horses he already owned.

She was pleased at how well she had settled to farm life. Everything that had appeared so daunting to her at first was now familiar. Breakfast was ready, and she expected James to come for it soon, after checking on the animals. Just the thought of him filled her with goose bumps, and her thoughts flashed back to the wedding night when they were alone for the first time.

"Would you like something to eat before going to bed?" he had posed, noticing how nervous she looked. Shaking her head, Fiona searched for something to steal away attention from her. James seemed to understand, as he had shown her to their room, leaving her alone to prepare for bed.

She smiled at the memory of their first night together, unaware he stood watching her, leaning on the door.

"Penny for your thoughts," he said, making her jump a little.

"Oh it's nothing, just a few memories crossing my mind."

"Must be good ones," he teased, an amused look on his face.

His searching gaze made her blush, and she went to the kitchen to get breakfast.

They ate quietly together, no longer any tension between them. All that existed now was silent intimacy borne out of their knowledge of each other in the past few days.

"So what plans do you have for the day?" he asked, setting down his fork with a satisfied smile. "I will be working on the kitchen garden most of the day. I need to make sure we have abundant supply in the coming months."

"That's great. Considering we are expecting good rains next season, you could do quite a lot with that patch at the back," he encouraged her. The fact that she had someone supporting her in all she did served as inspiration to her. Even now, sitting across him at the table, Fiona felt herself warming up under his keen gaze.

Without saying anything, James got up on his feet to take her hand. She went to him willingly, enjoying the feel of his arms around her.

"I cannot begin to tell you how much joy you have brought my way. Thank you for turning my life around for the better," he said as he pulled her even closer for a kiss.

"I better get going now or the poor animals might starve to death," he said, and released her reluctantly to go tend to the animals.

A silent prayer on her lips, Fiona pondered on the way destiny had turned out in her favor. Unlike some of the girls from the East who came to get married to men known only by letter, she was blessed to have found a god-loving man for a husband. Eyes turned heavenwards in thanks, she stepped out to yet another day on the farm.

Chapter Nine-More Trouble

They had been married five months when disaster struck again. Fiona was working on the farm when gunshots rang out in the distant. Immediately on the alert, she ran towards the house to lock herself in. James had advised her to run to safety should she sense any such danger. Heart beating wildly in her chest, she clutched the door latch, wondering where her husband was.

James was working at the edge of the property when several men approached. Immediately upon seeing them, he knew they were up to no good. One of them called out as they got closer, making known their intentions.

"Howdy farmer. What fine animals you have there," he said.

James knew they were after the horses, something he would not give up without a fight. It didn't matter they were four of them, as he carried his gun around most of the time now.

"How can I help you gentlemen?" he inquired. He was reaching for his gun when a shot rang out, hitting him on the shoulder. Realizing time was no longer on his side, he fired back. In the exchange, two of the gangsters were seriously injured and went running into the dark. Unfortunately, the men took three of his horses with them.

Worried about Fiona, he headed home. But as he walked, the pain grew stronger. Slowly shooing the remaining animals homewards, he made his way in the dark, teeth tightly clenched in pain. Fiona heard the commotion outside, and peering between the curtains, caught sight of James. Frightened by the way he was clutching at his shoulder, she rushed to him.

"Oh my, you are bleeding! What happened to you?" she asked, helping him inside the house.

"I ran into the outlaws again," he said weakly. Without wasting further time she went to get warm water and cloth to stop the bleeding. James was obviously in great pain, and he grimaced each time she touched him.

"Quickly, get the herbs Charlotte showed you and put them on the wound,'' he said weakly.
It was all she could do not to cry seeing her husband in pain. Never had she handled a gunshot before, and it was a scary incident for her. Especially as the casualty was someone she loved so dearly.

"What else should I do? Please tell me, James," she said to him. Hearing the panic in her voice, he reassured her that the pain would subside with time.

Trying to make him as comfortable as could be in the circumstances, she helped him to bed. Soon he was fast asleep, leaving her to go and lock up the animals. That night was spent nursing the wound as his temperature rose, signaling possible infection. By the following morning, his breath was coming in rapid gasps. With nothing else to do, Fiona hurried to get Bobby for assistance. She burst through the front door to find the couple just getting up.

"You have got to help me, Bobby," she said between gasps. Charlotte heard her and came running from the kitchen. Concern written all over her face, she went to her side.

"What is the matter Fiona?" she asked. Tears rolled freely down Fiona's face as she attempted to explain.

"It's James, he was shot last night and is in pain," she blurted out. At the mention of her brother's name, Charlotte let out a loud scream. Bobby quickly gathered himself so they could leave together. Soon the three of them arrived back at the farm to find James groaning with pain.

"He needs to see the Doctor immediately. That wound needs to be looked at," said Bobby. Together they helped James into the buggy, leaving Charlotte behind to tend to the animals, who had not been fed that morning.
Watching her husband roll around in pain as she held onto him, it was as if Fiona could feel his pain. Dabbing sweat off his face, she silently prayed for recovery. Never had Fiona thought she could feel the pain of another the way she did that of her husband. They were lucky to find the doctor already in, and immediately James was put on the examining table.

"Looks like the bullet is lodged in his shoulder. I will need to extract it to facilitate healing of the wound," the doctor said. "You should all leave the room now. I'll let you know when it's done."

The procedure seemed to take forever, but finally the doctor opened the door and invited Fiona in to see James. His shoulder now wrapped in a bandage, he attempted to smile through the pain.

"I feel better now, so no need to look so alarmed. I am sure I will be up and around in no time at all," he said faintly. They helped him back onto the buggy and slowly made their way home, Bobby driving carefully to avoid inflicting further pain. Fiona was then left to nurse him back to health, now that he was out of danger.

Chapter Ten-Recovery

With the responsibility of running the farm squarely on her, Fiona barely had time for anything else. Charlotte dropped by often to see how James was getting on, and she was grateful for the company. James was regaining strength quickly, and Fiona took time to check on him regularly throughout the day in the midst of her chores.

"I am not so bad now, you don't have to worry about me," he told her one afternoon after she found him sitting up in bed. He looked much better with a stubble of beard on his face, she noticed.

"You gave me quite a scare there, James. I don't know if I would have been able to cope had anything happened to you."

A small smile played on his face on hearing her words. Fiona had been hovering around him like a mother hen, taking care of him. James knew he was lucky to have married such a caring wife, and the incident only served to confirm to him what a treasure she was to him. He reached out for her then, with his good hand to draw her closer, and she enjoyed the feel of his arm around her one more.

"I have missed you while I have been sick. Damn those scoundrels for intruding on our lives the way they did," he said, taking in the smell of her hair. Already Fiona could feel her heart starting to race inside her chest at being so close to him. The two cuddled for a while, but had to stop after a sharp pain shot through his shoulder, causing him to flinch.

She jumped back, sensing his pain. They would have to wait for him to heal completely before attempting anything more strenuous. Smiling apologetically, James let out a sigh and then fell back onto the bed.

There was much to be done on the farm, so time flew fast, and soon James was back on his feet. "I wish there was something we could do about these outlaws. In these parts, we get such attacks every once in a while, and have slowly resigned to the fact," he told her one afternoon.

"Do you mean that we should live expecting to be attacked anytime? Isn't it scary you might have lost your life in the attack?" Fiona asked.
For a moment he was silent, reflecting on what she had just said.

"The local sheriff has made several attempts to curb the menace, but since we are close to the mountains it still happens often," he said, unwilling to pursue the topic further. He had other thoughts on his mind right then, and security was not one of them.

"C'mon, let's go to bed now. It has been a long day today."

As always, they knelt down together beside the bed to give thanks to God for preserving his life. It was comforting to know they could trust Him to sustain them in the future, as their hope was in Him.

Chapter Eleven- Then Came a Surprise

The next few weeks were a busy time for them. Most farmers in the area were waiting for winter to come to an end so that they might start to prepare their farms. All was going well for them until one day when Fiona went to the market, where she met some women from church.

The two ladies were older than her. She recognized them as some of those who had come to help Charlotte out during the preparations for her wedding. On seeing her, she noticed them look at each other in a funny manner. Fiona did not give much thought to it, and politely called out greetings to the two as she passed.

"Good morning Fiona, how are you doing?" one of them answered as the other remained staring at her curiously.

What could be the matter with those two, she wondered. Picking up what she needed, she came upon them again, and stepped to the side, listening. "That poor girl, only just recently married to James. If she only knew just who is on the heels of her husband."

So that was why the two women had looked at her in such a funny way earlier? Determined to find out as much as she could about their story, she lingered around them a while longer.

"That James should know better than to encourage the attentions of someone who has abandoned her own husband. This will not go well, especially should his new wife find out." Fiona had heard enough, and decided to get on her way. More confused than angry, she wondered who the woman in question was. How might it be that James would have eyes for another woman?

"Oh God, not this. I can't bear to think my marriage might be under risk already. Please step into the matter and guard the heart of my husband," she prayed softly.

James was busy with the farm chores when she got home. Seeing him looking so hard at work, it was difficult for her to reconcile it with what she had heard about him. Wishing she could dismiss it altogether, she knew she would know no peace until the truth was out. Thinking it might be wiser to wait before saying anything to him, she prayed to God for the patience.

"You are unusually quiet today. Might there be something that happened while you were away?" James inquired at dinner, eyes fixed on hers. Not sure whether to mention what she had heard, she decided to take a bit more time with it. There would be no use throwing it into his face while not sure it was the truth.

"I am fine, James. Just a bit tired from the trip today."

"Oh dear, I am sorry to hear that. Maybe I can go get groceries next time? I really wouldn't mind, you know."

The way he spoke almost made her forget her fears. But the doubts that had been planted were still there, niggling at the back of her mind.

"I wouldn't have you do that. I enjoy those trips to the market, as it gives me a chance to catch up with the news," she answered him.

They went to bed soon after. Tired from working hard on the farm, James fell asleep, leaving her alone with her thoughts.

Who is the woman those two were talking about, and how true is what they said? If indeed it is true she is after him, has he done anything to encourage her? Looking at the man who lay beside her, she had difficulty reconciling him to what she had overheard. He seemed so innocent; she prayed it was a lie.

The next few days were tense for Fiona. She had considered going to see Charlotte, perhaps throw a hint about her concerns. But every time the thought popped into her mind, she pushed it off, preferring instead to ignore it.

The chance to confront James with the issue occurred one day as she was clearing the breakfast dishes. Being a cold morning, she had a fire going in the kitchen and stayed close to it for warmth. James was in a playful mood, stealing up to her at every chance. He had just bent down to nuzzle her neck when she let it out.

"I wonder at times, James. With your looks, how come you were not attracted to any woman around?" she teased him playfully. James seemed startled by her question, taking time to answer her. When he did, it was to surprise her with the answer.

"To tell you the truth, I have had a number of women show interest in me. None of them even came close to catching my interest in any way." She thought for a while whether to continue the conversation, then deciding to keep things between them open, went ahead.

"I have been meaning to ask you something, James. Something I overheard some women talk about at the market," she began, shooting him an inquiring look in the process. James stared ahead stoically, waiting for her to go on. "Is it true there is a woman who has been following you around even after we got married?" she asked in a rush.

James could not hide the surprise on his face at hearing her ask the question.

"Actually, you are right about that. I have been meaning to tell you about it for a while, but saw no reason to since I am not the one going after her. But I am not interested in anyone but you."
"When were you going to tell me about it, James? Didn't we agree to keep no secrets from each other?" Fiona went on, visibly angry.

At this, James straightened up to face her.
"Ok, fine. I will tell you. I have known Maggie over the years and at some point even did business with her ex-husband. The two were married for a while before they began having issues. Several of us were called to try and bring understanding between them, and I was one of them." He paused for a moment, gathering his thoughts.

"Nothing any of us did could help them stay together," he continued. "The two went different ways, eventually bringing their marriage to an end. Maggie used to come by at times. Just to say hello. That stopped however, after she learned I was getting married. She would not talk to me for a while after I told her. I think she felt angry, but I never led her on. I was never interested in her in that way.''

At last the truth was out, but it also left Fiona with a number of questions. If indeed he had nothing to hide, why had he not mentioned anything about this to her? Was it possible he, too, harbored feelings for the woman? Unable to hold off any longer, she belted out her thoughts to him.

"You were keeping things from me James. That's not fair, you know. I wonder who this woman is who has feelings for you," she said, storming out of the room.

"What are you getting all worked up about? I told you, that woman means nothing to me. Will you believe me or those gossiping women you overheard talking?" he shouted at her.

"Thanks to them, I found out your little secret. You ought to feel real bad about keeping things like that from your wife. That is lying, James." Stomping off, she made her way to bed.

Perhaps Lucy was right; she too had encountered a liar. Unable to bear the thought, she got into bed and covered her head to cry herself to sleep. James did not follow her, choosing instead to sleep on the couch. The two had just had their first fight, and an ugly one at that.

Chapter Twelve – Lonely Times

The first thing Fiona noticed upon getting up was how much her head hurt. It felt as if it was coming apart, drumming ceaselessly as she got out of bed. She noticed James's side of the bed was untouched, and then went to look out the window. Winter would soon come to an end, and the weather was starting to warm up. She wished that was the case with her heart too, as right then it felt cold with betrayal.

The living room was empty when she got there, and there were no signs of him anywhere. Heading to the kitchen to start breakfast, she still hoped he might be somewhere in the house. After having coffee, she got started on the house chores, wondering where he may be. When dinner time approached with no signs of James, she got worried, thinking something might have happened to him.

She spent a fitful night, not knowing what might have happened to James.

"He was not there when I got up yesterday. He left with no word, and haven't heard from him since," she explained to Charlotte early the next morning. The older woman seemed surprised, thinking things over for a while.

"Did the two of you argue about something?" she asked, probing eyes on Fiona.

She knew there was no way would she be able to lie to Charlotte, and so she owned up.

"As a matter of fact, we did, Charlotte. It had to do with that woman Maggie."

Charlotte clapped hands to her head on hearing that. "Oh, that woman. You mean she is still following my brother around? I have personally warned her off him, but she seems bent on pursuing him. Have you met her yet?" she asked, looking tired all of a sudden.

"You know about her, too? Tell me, Charlotte, what exactly has been going on between her and my husband?"

The older woman struggled with what to tell her, and then came to a decision.
"Why don't we take a seat in the living room? Perhaps it is time for us to talk."

In the living room, Charlotte continued. "Maggie is not the kind of woman I would be proud to be associated with. She abandoned her husband so as to follow her randy ways. Few of us like to associate with her, and only a few remain friends with her." She paused for a while, gathering her thoughts.

"I am surprised to hear she is still after James. He should know better than to entertain her," she said with a hint of anger in her voice.

Not knowing what to think, Fiona remained silent, trying to take in what she had heard. By the time she got up to leave, one thing was clear to her. They would work things out as soon as James got back home. Hoping he would be there when she arrived, she was disappointed to find the house still empty.

The days she spent by herself at home were the most traumatizing she had known. At times she wondered if James might have run into the arms of the woman she had heard of. She missed him, and longed for him to get back home to her. The days were filled with chores needing to be done now that she was by herself. And when she went to bed each night, it was to lie awake wondering where James might be.

"God, please watch over my husband and keep him out of harm's way," she prayed each night. On the other side of town, James sat on the single bed in the room he had taken for a few days.

Unable to understand how the woman he loved might think so ill of him; he had decided to take a break. Why couldn't his wife understand that Maggie was just a woman he knew?

Each day he stayed in that room he hoped would be his last. Yet he found himself still there when night came the following day. He would have to face up to the situation and go back home. He was just not ready to face her yet. The fact that she did not trust him hurt him more than he could stand.

He missed her, and the thought that something might happen to her while he was away almost had him running back, but steeling himself he stayed. He had to be ready when he went back home, no matter how long it took.

Back home, Fiona had just began a new day without her husband and was worried. Four days had gone by since the fight, and having heard nothing from him, she wondered what was on his mind. She was getting ready to go feed the horses when she noticed a buggy approach. Thinking the person might have news about James, she rushed to the front door to check.

The woman stepping out of the buggy did not seem familiar to her. The minute she saw her, alarm went through her mind, and she steeled herself for what was coming. The woman seemed very sure of herself, knocking loudly at the door. Fiona went to open it, and then stood staring at her.

"How can I help you?" she asked. The other woman looked her up, and then asked to see James.

"Who are you, and what do you want with my husband?" Fiona asked, not bothering to hide her irritation. The other woman sneered, and a short laugh escaped her lips.

"Tell me where James is. I am not here to pick a fight with his little wife." So saying, she made as if to enter the house, but Fiona blocked her way. "James is not here, and you don't have any business going inside."

The two women stood staring at each other at the door, neither willing to let up.

"Maggie! What are you doing here?" The voice that called out did not sound too pleased. James had made his way home, and now stood looking at the woman with disdain. Fiona stepped back, waiting to see what would happen.

"Oh, there you are James! Your little wife will not let me in to the house," the woman said, pouting at James. He took a step towards her then and grasped her hand.

"You have no reason coming here to bother my wife. What is it you want from me?" he asked, shaking her arm.

Maggie grimaced. "Ouch. You're hurting me! What has gotten into you James? Has this little vixen stolen your mind?" She threw a nasty look Fiona's way.

"That little vixen you see there is my wife. I married her because I love her. Nothing you say or do can change that fact, and now if you will excuse me, it is time for you to go."
Maggie looked as if she had been hit and turned to leave, not bothering to say goodbye. James took Fiona in his arms, and together they walked in to the house.

"I hope I made my stand clear enough," he told her as they got ready for bed.
"More clear than I had hoped. That woman is a true bother." There was no further talking, as man and wife began to recover the time they had lost. Being apart had helped each appreciate the other more than they had imagined.

Later in the night, Fiona cuddled close to her husband, grateful he was home. God had stepped in once again, to bring to light what might have brought problems to them.

"You know, I prayed God to keep you safe all the time you were away," she whispered. James drew her close, breathing softly in her hair.

"I missed you so, Fiona. I only needed time to think things over on my own."

Happy with his explanation, she went to sleep in his arms.

Chapter Thirteen- Help a Friend

The next time she went to the market, Fiona had James with her. The two were back at ease, having resolved the issue with Maggie. Bouncing happily along, they were well on the way when she spotted Lucy.

The girl was walking by herself, head bowed down. She had a small bag strapped on her back, and seemed to have a lot on her mind. When she saw her, Fiona asked her husband to stop the buggy. Stepping down, she went to find out what was going on with her friend.

Lucy started crying the minute she saw her. She was on her way back home, she said, being unable to hold up any longer. She didn't even have enough fare to get there, as she had not told him she was going away.

"You mean George has no idea you are leaving?" Fiona asked her. "You better come on with us, Lucy. You can't go on looking like that. Why don't you let me get a few things at the market then we can go back home and talk things over?" Lucy stopped crying, looking up at her. "Really? Do you mean that?"

"Of course I do, Lucy. I am sure James does not mind." Fiona said, turning to her husband. James nodded sadly, happy to help.

The two women headed back home together, leaving James to finish off his business in town. Lucy looked better now, even though unable to hide her sadness. As soon as they got to the house, Fiona sent Lucy to her room to freshen up, and then went to start lunch. By the time they were done cooking, Lucy seemed calmer.

"Tell me what happened with you and George," Fiona offered. "What made you want to leave and go back home?"

Lucy fidgeted for a while before she spoke.

"He is not what I wanted, Fiona. When I came here, I was hoping for a man who would love me for me. He trashed all that, thought, openly going after other women instead." She was close to tears as she spoke.

Watching the other girl looking so unhappy, Fiona considered what to tell her. She understood well the feeling of being pushed aside by one's husband. Anxious for a way to help her, she continued with the questions.

"Have you tried talking to him about how that makes you feel? Perhaps he might have a reason for his actions."

A resigned look on her face, Lucy went on.

"The only time I asked him about it, he laughed openly at me and then told me to stop imagining things. He would never admit to it."

"Are you sure of what you think, Lucy? How do you know he is seeing other women?"
Lucy seemed disturbed by where the conversation was heading. She had not expected that many questions.

"I have only heard about it from the neighbors," she said, sounding subdued.
James came in then, making their conversation stop for a moment. Fiona went to get him lunch, then together with her friend began doing chores around the house.

One night a few days later, Fiona prayed again for her friend before going to bed. Ever since Lucy came to live with them, she had been spending time praying for her and her husband. Her prayer was for God to bring reconciliation their way, as she had sensed stubbornness in her friend. Once she was done, she climbed into bed with James, grateful they were happy together.

"You know, I have a feeling your friend should seek out her husband. Perhaps there is hope for the two of them still," James said to his wife as they lay together in bed.
"I have the same feeling. Lucy can be stubborn at times."

"Time will tell, Fiona. Keep praying for her and you never know."
On a Sunday a week later, the two woke up to find her gone. Lucy had left to go back to George to seek reconciliation. Together, Fiona and James read the note she had left.

I have learnt a lot from you two. At times words are not necessary.

Seeing her prayers had borne fruit, Fiona went to share the news with James before they got ready to go to church.

"She has gone to be with her husband, James. Our prayers for Lucy were answered."

James's face lit up at hearing that.

"I told you she would go back. It was only a matter of time," he said.

The two then left to go to church, happy to have made a difference.

With winter almost over, people were making plans for the coming plantings.

"I can't wait to get started on the farm again. This time, I am determined to make a good living off the land for the two of us," James said. Happy to hear how positive he sounded, Fiona encouraged her husband.

"I am sure we will pull through. God will make a way out for us, James."

One day as the two sat chatting after having lunch, they were surprised to see a buggy pull up. Lucy stepped out, accompanied by a man who could only be George. The two walked up, calling out greetings as they came.

"We are sorry for stealing up on you unannounced. My wife here would not give me peace until we came," George said.

James was on his feet to welcome the two to the house. Beaming, he ushered them in.

"No use apologizing. We are happy to have you over," he said.

The two women disappeared into the kitchen to catch up while making tea.

"Watching you and James so happy together made me realize how much I was missing," Lucy said. "I could not stand the thought I was letting others win by leaving my husband, and so decided to go back and work at our marriage. I am so glad I did, as we have renewed our vows to each other and I am more accepting of him."

Then, before Fiona could say anything, she went on eagerly.

"You know what else? I just discovered I am expecting a baby. I could not sleep without coming over to tell you," Lucy said, running a hand over her stomach.

"Wonderful! I am so happy for the two of you. God has indeed favored you," Fiona told her friend, beaming across at her.

"So now that you know what news I brought over, I hope you will keep it to yourself until we are gone," said Lucy, giving her friend a wink. The two women walked back to the living room, carrying fresh juice and snacks.

"You two seem to have had fun in there. I wonder what you were talking about," James joked, a cheeky look on his face. He had taken the chance to know George better, and the two got along very well.

"Nothing really. We were just catching up on each other" Fiona said with a smile at Lucy. When the time came for them to leave, George helped a beaming Lucy back on the buggy, and then climbed in beside her. They waved as they left, looking happy together.

Watching them go, Fiona thought of the thin line between giving up and finding happiness once again. Forgiveness had a role to play in relationships, without which they might not work. "I sure am glad we had something to do with their getting back together. Those two make a great couple," James said, putting his arm around his wife. Fiona agreed, anxious to share Lucy's secret with him.

With a bright smile on her face she turned to look at him. "They not only got back together, but also have something to show for it. Lucy is going to have a baby."

James beamed, happy at the news. Then smiling at her he said, "A challenge, I suppose?"

Chapter Fourteen- Happy at Last

The rain beating against the windows woke Fiona. The sound of it made her edge closer to her sleeping husband, causing him to stir in his sleep. She lay quietly for a while, not wanting to rouse him during this peaceful time.

She was grateful for the love of her husband. For the first time, she understood what it meant to love another so entirely, despite the flaws. Never before had she thought she could care as much for someone as she did him.

As if he sensed her mood, he turned in his sleep, drawing her close. "Why are you not asleep?" he drawled, voice drowsy with sleep.
She basked in his warmth, enjoying the sound of the rain.

"The rain woke me up."

He drew her even closer, leaving no room between them. Nuzzling into her neck, he said to her, "You know what they say about falling asleep to the sound of the rain?"

Giving her no chance to answer, he took her in his arms again, this time to hold her through the night. One day not long after the rainy night, Fiona began to notice she tired rather easily. Blaming it on the hard work on the farm, she gave it little thought, until she began feeling sick in the mornings.

Charlotte learned of it and came over to see her, but after spending a while with her had a big smile on her face.

"You have nothing to worry about, Fiona. You are not sick but are with child," she said, glimmer in her eyes. Fiona sat motionless for some time before she flew into the arms of the older woman. This was the best news she had in a long time and she could barely wait to share it with James.

"What? I am going to be a mother? How gracious God is to me!" she said, almost breaking down. "Indeed he has been good to you two. I am so happy you now have something to look forward to together," Charlotte told her, readying to leave.

Left alone, Fiona fell on her knees in thanksgiving to God for the added blessing.
When finally the two lay in bed that night, she told him the good news about the baby she was expecting.

"Indeed God is good to us," James said, pulling her close. "I have never been more blessed."
Nor I, thought Fiona, smiling.

The End

FREE GIFT

Just to say thanks for purchasing my book, I'd like to gift you a Best Selling FREE Mail Order Bride Audiobook <u>100% FREE!</u>

Please GO TO

<u>http://cleanromancepublishing.com/mobgift</u>

And get your FREE gift

Thanks for being such a wonderful client.

Please Check out My Other Works

By checking out the link below

http://amazon.com/author/faith.johnson

Thank You

Many thanks for taking the time to buy and read through this book.

It means lots to be supported by SPECIAL readers like YOU.

Hope you enjoyed the book; please support my writing by leaving an honest review to assist other readers.

With Regards,

Faith Johnson

Printed in Great Britain
by Amazon